SANDS OF TIME

A
COLLECTION OF
THOUGHT-PROVOKING STORIES

BEATRICE C. SNIPP

Typeset in Minion Pro

Editing, design, typesetting and publishing by UK Book Publishing

www.ukbookpublishing.com

ISBN: 978-1-913179-56-4

FOREWORD

TO ANYONE WHO MIGHT READ THIS BOOK.

These few short stories are not written to entertain or pass away a short train journey.

They are written to make your little grey cells work (Hercule Poirot).

Hopefully they might make you think a little longer after reading.

On time, space and human companionship to name but a few.

For anyone that might have a question on the stories, good or bad (no swearing please), you can find me on:

beatricecsnipp@gmail.com

I welcome any comments or thoughts you may have on any of the stories printed.

SANDS OF TIME

CONTENTS

THE SMELL OF DEATH

HOW DO I START TO TELL MY STORY!

I was eight, a normal boy playing with friends and neighbours, fighting and generally being a nuisance to my mum.

While picking blackberries with my mum and two older brothers to make blackberry and apple pie, one of my brothers pushed me into a bramble bush.

In my efforts to extricate myself I got even further enmeshed into the patch of brambles. By the time my mother pulled me clear of the brambles, my face was awash with blood.

Grabbing my mother, I remember screaming, "Mummy, I cannot see."

My mother held my arms so I could not scratch my eyes on the way to the hospital in the ambulance.

I cried more than I have ever done or will ever do again.

The verdict when I eventually left the ophthalmic hospital I had been transferred to was that I would never be able to see again. The brambles had irrevocably ruined my sight when entering them and I had tried rubbing my eyes to get to get them out.

I am thirty-two now and have come to terms with my disability many years ago.

They say your senses heighten so that they cover the lost sense.

In my case my sense of smell became incalculably superior to any of the others.

This took until my middle twenties before I realised how unrivalled they had become.

I detract from my story.

As I reached my early teens, I began to notice that I could smell things others could not. Not just the normal things like others would and could, but things I could not understand.

Take for example when visiting my nan in hospital. She was in for a routine operation on her legs. As soon as I walked into the ward I tugged at my mum's hand and complained of the smell.

Mum told me to hush, it was only the disinfectant they used and all hospitals smelt that way.

We sat at the bed and all the time the smell was getting stronger. I moved around the bed and the aroma was so pungent I asked my mum if we could leave.

Eventually we did and Mum cursed me for showing her up and stressing Nan out before her operation.

We visited Nan two days later after the operation and she was very cheerful.

The smell was still there but more astringent, so strong. I asked if I could wait in the waiting room.

My nan passed away a week later due to complications during the operation, my mum said.

I never saw my nan again, but at the funeral the smell had been replaced with an aromatic tingling to my nostrils.

Gradually over the next ten years I came to realise that I could smell death in others.

How do I tell them, how could I tell them? The strength of the odour determined how long they had to live.

I finally came to accept – no, appreciate – what this gift was when I was in my early twenties.

Walking down the High Street one day cane in hand, I had to stop; the aroma I had come to associate with death was so overpowering it was making me gag.

Before I could clear my throat a loud screech of brakes, a heavy thud, a noise like a sack of potatoes being thrown through a glass window, crying all around from many vocal cords and shocked onlookers.

To my astonishment the acrid smell in my nose had

gone and been replaced with the aroma I had become accustomed to, the afterlife. An accident involving a bus and a small child had just occurred and I could do nothing to stop it.

Over the years I accustomed myself to this second insight into smell and never told anyone so as not to alarm them or that they might think me a freak.

I am now thirty-four and sitting on a train going for Sunday lunch at my brother's.

The smell has been with me for over a week now and is becoming ever stronger.

I have not come to terms with the meaning of this, but I shower constantly. It does not get rid of the smell but it makes me feel better.

I hear a loud crash and the smell dissipates; the aromatic smell returns.

I feel my body floating. I see pictures again? I do not understand – my eyes see again; I drift away and upwards from the scene below. A train is on its side crumpled with people walking around in a daze.

I see it all and feel an elixir of being alive again with all my senses.

It's then I realise that I am not there but above, as my vision fades to a dim glow then brightens as if standing on the sun.

I cannot explain it. As it is for you to work out what you believe in.

As for me, that would be telling.

?   /

THE UNWANTED SOLDIER

HIS FINGERS CARESSED THE SANDWICH.
He had not eaten for days; in fact, he could not remember when he had last consumed a proper meal.

Tired, weary and hungry, Jake had found this nearly whole sandwich three quarters of the way down a rubbish bin, just past the recently regurgitated McDonald's and vodka that someone had left the night before.

Brushing off the diced carrots that had been liberally sprayed all over the bin by a passer-by and not giving an iota of a thought to the smell, Jake pulled back the cellophane top that had been replaced and had kept the diced carrots off of it. A bite had been taken out of one end. Jake could see it was either a teenager or a lady as the bite was small and round.

As he pulled it out and looked at it before eating it – the smell is funny! Jake thought to himself. Reading the top… Coronation chicken, um! Cannot remember ever eating one of these.

He placed it between his lips and bore down with the

full force of his gums.

Jake had no teeth – they had all been pulled by the Japanese while fighting for King and country during the Second World War. Not in a nice way but under interrogation.

Passers-by looked on as Jake sat on the bench. Hair – or should I say what was left of it – hung on his shoulders like a withered tree's branches.

Alopecia had affected Jake since he joined the army – he was allergic to the uniform.

Since demob and twenty odd years later at the grand old age of forty-seven, Jake found himself moving from town to town. Too proud to beg or go to the labour exchange – or as we call it now the Job Centre.

Money was not a thing that worried Jake, his mind still thinking of his teeth being pulled one by one to find out troop movement in Burma.

The people walking past Jake looked, sniffed and hurriedly moved on with their oh so important lives.

Prime Minister Mr Wilson was just about to devalue the pound, by around 40%. Jake knew nothing and cared even less as he ate the sandwich and pushed the remainder into his mouth. A piece of chicken that was hanging from his gums was quickly pushed back in.

The Army had given Jake a set of ill-fitting dentures when he was repatriated from the prison camp. Four and a half stone, five foot ten and a broken man.

The teeth had been ditched soon after as Jake hated the feel of the badly fitting dentures. A foreign body in his mouth, too many thoughts drifted back to those times.

A real war hero was Jake, medals and citations galore. The George Cross was one of many. presented by Winston Churchill himself.

Then forgotten, yesterday's news; people wanted to forget the war, so did Jake.

It played on his mind and gave him unpleasant nights' sleep on the bench of his choice when the weather was fine.

Jake's heroism during his torture was thought to have saved countless lives but had ruined his. Would it have been better for Jake to have had a normal life and for children and men to die?

We will never know. Jake was found the next morning rigid. The autopsy said it was food poisoning.

Jake was just glad to be done with the dissipated life he had lived after being discharged.

The only way they knew who Jake was by the birthmark on his left buttock and his discharge papers that he still carried neatly folded in greaseproof paper stitched into his overcoat.

His regiment buried Jake with full military honours. As the most decorated war veteran ever in their regiment, he has a large inscription on his gravestone with his full roll of honours.

People came from his old regiment, from where he was born and his old teachers and schoolmates. They all spoke of him at the wake held after the ceremony.

Coronation chicken sandwiches were one of the items people consumed after the burial while reminiscing about old times.

That was yesterday's old news, people forget until it is time to dig them up for today's entertainment.

What would Jake have thought! Suffice to say his thoughts would not have been of the printable kind.

Where were they when he needed them? Like most people today, tied up in their own little world. until the world comes and hits them.

Rest in peace, Jake; many a man walks this Earth due to your heroism. Untold and unknown by many but me.

So, God Bless to you and your kind.

Next time you pass a tramp, think. Think! He had a life and you may be here due to him or her.

MY TROUSERS

I KNOW IT MIGHT SEEM STRANGE TO SOME PEOPLE, BUT I BUY ALL MY CASUAL JEANS AND TROUSERS AT CHARITY SHOPS.

To buy new I could spend easily between £20 and £40 a pair. A charity shop as little as £2.50 or as much as £6.00.

I could spend as much as is needed just by putting my hand into my pocket! Let me explain and go back a few weeks. I like tight jeans and the sort that has elastic in them. As they do not make them in a man's jeans I buy women's jeans as long as the zip is on the man's side. Now let me put you straight: I do not feel embarrassed by wearing them, just buying them.

I tend to look for a size 12 or 14 elasticated, slightly bell bottomed, with the zip on the right. The men's side; I will not entertain the zip on the left.

Anyway I detract from the story. I never try them on as I always wait until I get home. If for some reason I do not like them, or they do not fit, I can always take them back and donate them to a different charity shop from whence they came.

Having bought two pairs, one cord, the other denim, before going home I decided to have a coffee. Finishing the coffee and wishing I had brought the car into town, I made my way back just in time to see the end of the third Test against Australia. We lost by four wickets.

After making and eating a sandwich I decided to try the trousers on. They were a good fit except for the length, which does not matter as a seamstress two doors down takes them up for £5. Feeling pleased with myself, I tried the cords on. Beige, slightly belled and a little loose at the waist, nothing that a belt would not fix.

Putting my hands in either pocket to hold them up to get a feel of the length, I found a piece of crumpled paper in the right pocket. I pulled it out and threw it on the table next to my empty plate.

Deciding to keep both pairs, I placed them back in the bag and picked up the crumpled piece of paper. The paper was rolled up quite tight, but I soon realised that it was not a receipt from a shop but a £20 note.

I was now in a quandary: do I take the £20 back to the shop or keep it? While thinking I took the trousers back out to see if there were any other bits with the previous owner's address on, as they certainly had not been checked before putting out on display. Checking both back pockets, one after the other, nothing in them, left front nothing in there, fidgeting around in the right front with my hand I felt another crumpled piece of paper.

Withdrawing it slowly, to my amazement it was another £20. Unfolding this one and putting it neatly with the other one on the table, I then put my hand inside of the pocket again and pulled out another £20 note.

Time and time again I put my hand into the pocket and every time a £20 note came out. Fifteen minutes passed and the table was awash with £20 notes.

I sat in a daze at the table and quite honestly I did not know what to do. I began to count them; £3780 was the grand total.

It is impossible to explain something that you yourself find unbelievable. Checking each note to find a discrepancy, some were new, some old, some torn, some worn, all with a different number, none the same.

My first stupid thought was they had belonged previously to a magician and it was all a trick. Then I realised that the stack of notes I had was four inches thick, which would certainly have been noticed at some time by someone.

Many hours later after several bouts of checking the pocket and finding a £20 note on every occasion, intermittently having a brandy to help my nerves and increasing the notes on the table which overflowed onto the floor, I eventually fell asleep on the settee.

Waking with my eyes a little blurred with too much alcohol from the night before, I seemed to remember a dream about £20 notes.

Unsteadily standing and drawing the curtains, gazing out on a lovely spring morning, I could not get over how real the dream had been. Rubbing the sleep from my eyes, I turned to make a cup of tea in the kitchen.

The sight before me is somewhat hard to explain – if you can imagine being in a small room and someone had cut up tens of thousands of pieces of paper. Thrown them up in the air and had a mini hurricane. That was my first instant impression, that lasted all of two seconds.

The table was covered in piles, the floor was covered several inches thick in places. So was the sofa that I had slept on. Wiping the notes off the chair, I sat down and tried to think what to do.

Had I had an aberration the night before and robbed a bank and could not remember? I told myself not to be so stupid and began to count them… £47,120.

Now what do I do? Do I try to bank them, take them back to the charity shop and say I found them in the pocket, or are they all counterfeit?

I put my hand in the pocket and drew out another £20 note.

So I decided to put all the money into a plastic bag and go to the bank. They were not due to open for an hour or so, so I took myself into a local cafe just across from the bank to have a coffee and a bacon sandwich.

Realizing I had brought no money with me I put my hand into my pocket of the trousers I was now wearing so as not to lose them and pulled out a £20 note and gave it to the person the other side of the counter.

"Sorry I have not got change, you are the first one in." Before they could finish, I gestured for them to keep the change as I had won on the lottery. Retiring to a table in the bay window to await my bacon sandwich, I could not stop looking at my wristwatch.

I left the cafe at least fifteen minutes before the bank opened as you become convinced that everyone is staring at you and your bag.

I was first in at the bank when the doors opened. Walking straight up to the enquiries desk, I handed her a £20 note from my pocket and asked if it was a genuine note.

She looked at me and asked if there was a reason why I would not think it was genuine.

Thinking to myself what was I doing here, I pulled another one from my pocket then another until her little table was covered.

By this time I had gained the attention of all the staff behind the shatterproof glass counter and the customers who were standing in line to be served.

Another older employee had walked over and was standing behind the enquiries desk. The lady gathered up the notes and placed a rubber band around the money after counting.

"There is £580 here, what would you like me to do with it, sir?"

The older man standing behind asked me if I would step into an adjoining room while he spoke to a colleague.

"Can I get you a hot drink?" I was asked.

"No, I have just had one thanks," I replied somewhat impolitely.

Shortly after, he came back with another man and apologised for not introducing himself and that the under manager, Mr Taylor, would like to speak to me.

"Sorry I did not get your name, Mr Taylor asked.

"Tony, Tony Bell, yes that is my name and no I am not an ice cream man."

"Can I ask where you got the money from that you seem

to think may be counterfeit?"

Looking and feeling a little stupid, I said my pocket, and at the same time emptying the contents of the plastic bag containing almost £50,000 onto the table, to his incredulity.

Mr Taylor sat down and looked more shocked than I had been the previous night, as I kept pulling £20 notes from my pocket until there was a knock at the door and two policemen entered.

I am not sure whose eyes bulged more, Mr Taylor's or the two policemen, as they saw a huge amount of money on the table as I tried to explain to them what had happened.

One of the officers left. I later found out that as the notes to all intents and purposes were legal tender they were not sure what course of action to take. So he radioed back to his station and asked for a detective for guidance on what action to take.

Shortly after, a detective arrived. Would I mind if I was escorted back to the station for further enquiries, he asked.

I will tell you something, you do not know how silly you feel being escorted from a bank with a bag of money by two burly policemen into their car and driven away with the lights and horns on at speed.

I cannot say that the police interview was any different from the bank meeting room, other than the seats were not padded and a further two thousand pounds were added to the kitty.

After countless demonstrations to a countless number of people, one of the detectives who had remained in the room throughout, asked me to take my trousers off and they would supply me with an orange boiler suit – if that was satisfactory to me.

This is how I found myself sitting at a table wearing an orange boiler suit with two policemen; my trousers on the table and each policeman in turn rifled through my pockets as though his hand was a ferret.

It was at this point that another person came into the small room and introduced himself as Detective Superintendent Field.

"I have been told the rudiments, but could you go over them one more time so that I can hear them first hand."

After a long and lengthy telling of my little story, Field picked up the trousers turning them inside out and then turning the pockets inside out.

"You are telling me that all that money came from these trousers, Mr Bell."

"No I am telling you it all came from the right pocket–" with no little annoyance on my part.

Again he put his hand inside the pocket and pulled it

inside out, then pushed it back and fumbled some more.

His face looked at me quizzically as though to say, he's having me on.

"Well, Mr Bell are you still sticking to your story?"

Now I was feeling more than a little annoyed – all this money that they had seen me pull out and still they did not believe me.

Grabbing the trousers from Field, I pulled note after note out, throwing them on the table. After the sixth note, Field grabbed the trousers back and again attacked the pocket with his hand to no avail.

"How did you do that?" All the time checking the pocket.

One of the policemen began to smile. "You dare laugh," Field said, sending the constable from the room.

After a few moments for Field to get his composure back, he looked me in the eye and spoke. "Are you telling me these are legal?"

"I am not telling you anything of the sort! That is why I went to the bank to find out."

"Well, Mr Bell I would like to keep the money and the trousers until we have contacted the Bank of England to clarify the situation, and also check the notes."

I took Field's offer of a lift home and felt relieved to leave the trousers and the money at the station.

They asked if I wanted to have the money counted in front of me, to which I declined – I was only too happy to go home.

Whilst I was sitting at home later that evening letting the day's events sift through my brain like mist through a chain link fence, the phone rang; it was the police station.

A voice introducing himself as Sergeant Withers informed me that if all was OK, they would like to pick me up at ten in the morning and transport me to the Bank of England. The trousers and money would accompany us and all out of pocket expenses would be forthcoming.

I found myself up early and was ready by 0830. I walked outside and waited the last fifteen minutes or so.

The car arrived a little early, an unmarked car with a driver and another man I had not met. The driver and his companion sat quietly in both front seats, the passenger holding a box on his lap which I presumed were my trousers and money.

Not a lot was said during the journey, which took an hour almost to the minute.

A very impressive building, the Bank of England. We drove down the side and entered into an underground car park. This is where I learnt that the car was not a police car but an official Bank of England courtesy car, and the driver worked for the Bank.

After a thorough security check with metal detectors and a manual search, we entered the lift and proceeded to the fifth floor.

Getting out of the lift, we walked along a narrow corridor, just wide enough for two people. We arrived at the end in front of two massive walnut doors, which were opened by someone inside like magic. Inside it was all wood and pictures of horses on the walls. The ends of the room were rounded to enhance the same curves on the large mahogany table, which had sixteen chairs pushed neatly under the table.

I was asked to sit at one end of the table and given the box containing the trousers and money.

It was explained by a rather dapper chap in a black coat, pin striped trousers and a very stiff collar that he kept tugging at. The box containing the items had been sent up the day before for inspection.

The dapper man went on explain that there was nothing unusual about the trousers and the notes were all legal, their issue being at various times over the last five years.

It seemed a silence had come over the room which seemed like an eternity but must have been only minutes.

The silence was broken by a middle-aged lady opening the door and announcing that Mr Pitt would see us now and ushered us through the door into a smaller room. Mr Pitt stood up from his desk and introduced himself as he stood up, walked around the desk and shook my hand.

It was then I realized three other people were sitting behind me against the wall.

Mr Pitt introduced each by name with their title and department, mentioning that he hoped I did not mind his colleagues being in attendance while we discussed the matter. I said I had no trouble with that at all.

"Well, Mr Bell, could you demonstrate what happens when you place your hand into the pocket please."

Taking the trousers from the box I proceeded to take note after note from the pocket and threw them on the table as all and sundry watched on.

Several times I was stopped and the trousers were checked and found to be empty. Eventually I was stopped and asked to leave the room while they discussed it further.

I was escorted to the in-house restaurant, that I must say had an array of meals on offer.

The only thing my escort said to me while I was eating my lunch in a rather terse voice was "how did you do that?"

I must say the food was extremely good and definitely

not a greasy spoon.

On finishing I was escorted back to the small room where all were still present.

Mr Pitt said, "We have no idea how or what happens when you put your hand into your pocket. The notes are all issued by us and are legal tender. We do not have the power to hold or confiscate the trousers or money. They are all legally yours, our legal department tell me.

"We must tell you that we have counted all the money from your trousers and it comes to a total of £74,260.

"I am empowered to ask you, that if you were to allow us to keep the money and the trousers as a gesture to yourself, we would furnish you with a cheque for £100,000 and of course a new pair of trousers.

"If you do not accept, we are at liberty to keep your goods for inspection, until we are satisfied that they are of no use to anyone.

"That could be disputed in court and cost a fortune in lawyers and time. I am sure you would be more than happy with the recompense which I have on my table awaiting your decision.

"Please do not see this as a bribe or heavy handed approach. Just a solution to the predicament we all find ourselves in. Please, if you feel that you would like to think about it for a while you are more than welcome to sit in a room or retire to the restaurant for a drink. We do need an answer today, I am sorry to inform you."

"No need to think it over," I replied. Almost before he had finished his sentence. I was never that happy with the trousers – they were too big – and as for the money I never wanted or asked for it.

"Good," Mr Pitt stammered, grabbing the trousers and putting them in the box with the money.

"Now if you would like to accompany me and my colleagues down to the basement, we will dispose of these."

We left the room all six of us, joined by a further four in the corridor. Making ten people. It took two separate journeys for all of us to get to the basement. Being joined by a further two people, one in a boiler suit. They were introduced to me as head of security and the head janitor.

Mr Pitt said that as the money and trousers could not be explained, they were to be incinerated together in the boiler.

The box containing the trousers and money were handed to the janitor, who opened the box so that everyone could see its contents. Opening a door on the boiler then a grate, he then pushed the box and its contents into the boiler. Everyone in turn looked through a small glass window to see the items being burnt.

"Thank you, Mr Bell, you will be taken back to your house now by car. A cheque and a new pair of trousers are in the car waiting for you," Mr Pitt said.

The journey did not seem to take as long going home, arriving at just gone six in the evening. I went to the kitchen to make a coffee, throwing the bag containing the cheque and trousers on the table.

"Had enough today," I said to myself. "Off to the pub for a Guinness." Which ended up as a long evening and too much Guinness. Nothing unusual there then.

I awoke in the morning to a thumping headache and a sore throat, so I decided to take a long shower then ring Billy to see if he was going to see the match on Saturday. Charlton were at home.

Sitting at the table, I thought I might as well try the trousers on. A pair of Marks & Spencer trousers which I duly put on. Same as the other ones, slightly too big. Putting my hands in the pockets I could feel a crumpled up piece of paper.

FOOD GLORIOUS FOOD

JOHN HAD A LOVE FOR PIZZA; COME TO THINK OF IT, JOHN HAD A LOVE FOR ANYTHING EDIBLE.

Perhaps that's why his lineage survived. His family motto may have been: See it kill it eat it.

Nevertheless they did survive, now food was bountiful and John was comparatively well off. So it was not just pizza John would tuck into with relish. It was anything that caught his eye or made his taste buds salivate copiously.

His urgency to eat was a sight to behold. It was nothing to get to the checkout of his local large supermarket after a slow and casual walk around every aisle. Picking up items and reading the label before putting them in his trolley.

Arriving at the checkout John would leave his heavily laden trolley near the till and get another trolley to load. When eventually arriving to pay, John would have two full trolleys. Both full to the brim.

On the top of one it was not unusual to find a half-eaten cooked chicken, an empty chocolate biscuit wrapper and a finished bottle of cola.

All left at the top of the food pile for the cashier to find and process. John was a regular and the cashiers all knew what to expect when John was next in the queue. Lo and behold anyone who was standing behind as this could and usually did take quite a while to bag up and put back in the trolley.

John found food more than a necessity, more a way of life. If he was not eating it, thinking of it or buying it, John was preparing it for himself, and of course while preparing it for himself a little snack.

Never an apple or banana – fruit was very low down on John's list, in fact so low down he never bought any.

A bit like his shoes when he wore them. In fact, John had not worn shoes for years, as he could not reach down to past his stomach to put them on. So he wore loose fitting slip-ons with no socks.

This day. Today that is. Is John's 36th birthday. It started like any other for the past few years in his uncluttered bungalow.

First thoughts were for breakfast, or should I say a snack while breakfast was being prepared.

A large bar of Bournville dark chocolate was a favourite. Also a large packet of sour cream crisps washed down with a few cans of cola.

John had only made it to the fridge door when he had a heart attack.

No one found John for over a week, the light from the fridge spotlighting John's features as he lay there, his last few seconds thinking of food and the pain it had made him feel over the years.

Would he have stopped if he had known?

Of course not, one does not apologise for one's own excesses unless you feel that you need to. In most cases the infringer believes his rights are being taken away with impunity.

They carried John out after, through the french windows which had to be removed to take John's body away.

No different to many others who eat, smoke, drink and generally indulge to excess.

Good on you, John, more for me to eat now!

XENOLITH

XENOLITH, A FRAGMENT OF ROCK FOUND EMBEDDED IN IGNEOUS ROCK TO WHICH IT DOES NOT BELONG.

Unusual words to bring into a conversation but Eric could and would.

It is not as though he had ever heard of them before. He looked them up in a dictionary and memorised them for use during the course of the next few days.

For example, xenolith he used to describe himself when he went to an away football match and found himself with the home supporters.

We all nodded and made tutting noises as if to say we knew what Eric was talking about.

Except for Martin – he would always ask Eric what the hell he was on about. Then followed a diatribe from Eric into Martin's ear on whatever the subject was.

This had gone on for years whenever we all met up for a drink. Eric would look up a word and somehow steer the conversation around to his way and bore us all stupid.

Our revenge was to come sweetly we hoped. It took myself and Chris months to learn our lines off by heart but eventually we did.

A few weeks after we had learnt our lines, we met in our local for a drink and a game of pool. We were waiting for the conversation to edge towards a precipice from which Eric could not return.

After a short discourse on the oceans and sea water, Chris interrupted. "Do you realise the pelagic white tipped shark has consumed, devoured and digested more than any other cartilaginous fish? Part of the Chondrichthyes family, I believe," Chris said looking at me.

"There are about four hundred known members to this family," I butted in. Adding that their skin was covered in denticles.

"The carcharodon carcharias, or to you, Eric, the great white, was widely thought of as the biggest but was not."

Chris interrupted. "That's right, the rhincodon typus, or to you, the whale shark is by far the biggest, but only eats plankton and small crustaceans."

Martin tried to butt in as I carried on. "Their eyes are highly sensitive to light and a membrane covers the eye when attacking to protect them."

Again Martin tried to get a word in edgeways but to no

avail. Chris was off again.

"Their sense of smell is so acute that one third of their brain is given up to interpreting its signals. They can also detect one part in a million of blood up to one mile away."

Eric tried to get into the conversation but could not. Chris and I kept a monotonous string of words relating to sharks for another five minutes, only stopping to breathe.

Chris was just about finishing with the lateral line along the body that picked up electrical current when Eric keeled over, spilling his drink over the pair of us.

Helping Eric to a chair as everyone else in the bar watched, we placed him carefully down and began to wipe the wet patches off our groin.

Eric seemed to recover very quickly so we replaced his Guinness on the table.

"Do you realize," Eric said, "the specific gravity of this pint is now read as the alcohol content. I find it hard to disassociate from the older way of reading strength of beer. Incontrovertibly inconvenient to one of my age to indiscriminate between the two."

I looked at Chris, he at me. We left Eric at the table and joined the others at the bar who were all laughing at us.

Do you know the person who has to have the last word, to feel mentally superior or could talk for England?

Well if you feel like us, we are just having a whip round for a one-way ticket to Syria and a T shirt with a picture of Donald Trump on the front and a bullseye target on the back.

It was either that or shoot him.

DEATH SO NEAR
BUT SO FAR

DEATH IS NOT A NORMAL THING TO TALK ABOUT WITH ONE'S EQUALS AT A PARTY. What the heck, it was 'J's party and 'J' was a special guy.

The four of us huddled together in the corner like four of Fagin's willing workers in Oliver Twist. Jabbering as we used to when we were known as the 'magic five' by our peers.

A glass of our favourite tipple in hand as always, grossly exaggerating what had happened since we last gathered.

The last gathering was at 'J's funeral and none of us felt like drinking on that morose and uncommunicative day.

His death was unexpected as death always is, even when you know or are expecting it.

There one day, gone the next; never the time or the thought to say what you really think of them, be it good or bad.

The unease when you assemble with the family and friends at the required meeting place before the funeral.

The shaking of hands, the cheek kissing and pleasantries you confide to one another. The telling of old stories that encapsulate the person you are about to say goodbye to for the final time.

Two weeks ago, at the funeral, seems such a long time already. Enough time to gather your thoughts but still the lump in your throat when you think of times spent and mischief created in times past.

You come to realize again and again as you grow older that you are not as immortal as you once thought.

That life is like an hourglass and the sand seems to drop quicker the nearer it has all gone.

Oh if only you could turn it over and start again. If only. If only.

The times we played cricket on a Sunday and our wives made the sandwiches.

'J' always drank too much in the sun and fell asleep one day while standing up umpiring, only to be woken by the bowler shouting 'HOW'S THAT' in his ear, and falling over again.

It is not always big things or comical things you remember as Trevor recalled.

We all played in the same local football team in our teens. Trevor and 'J' fought toe to toe and broke one another's noses over not being passed the ball. The referee was laughing so much he never even booked them.

Times were different then and in some ways better. None of us can remember the score though.

Another fight almost erupted after the match between the two of them and the rest of us, due in no certain fashion it cost us the match.

We could not stop poking fun at them all evening about the state of their noses.

The drinks are now nearly empty and we know we won't be having another.

We have this gathering every other Friday come what may. We just sit around our usual table and take the mick out of everyone who comes in.

It's funny there are only four of us now and I can sense an unease between us now that one of us has gone – perhaps 'J' was the glue holding us together.

Our combined age is almost 322 years. We know that the candle is almost extinguished. We just do not know whose will be the next to flicker and go out.

It's drawing late and it will be time to go home soon to bed. The young ones will stay up till all hours watching the telly, playing games or generally fooling around as we had done. It must be nice to be young again – or even 70.

I will lie in bed hoping my candle will be the next one to be doused.

I do not want to be the last one who lingers.

I hope I do not wake in the morning.

CATS

Kittens come and kittens go
Cats come and cats go
Fur clings where despair dwelt
Hope clings then moves forward
Some drop by the wayside
Some flourish like a rambling rose
That clings to the trellis for life
One puts a plaster where splints are called for
Then there are the people
Who try to evaluate each animal
Clean them feed them love them
Then see them go to a new home
A good home a loving home
To spend their remaining years in a land of milk and honey
With a person who respects them.

? /

DARKNESS

When the dark of the night meets the grey of the dawn
I will remember you
When the grey of the dawn meets the blue of the day
I will remember you
When the blue of the day meets the grey of the dusk
I will remember you
When the grey of the dusk meets the charcoal of evening
I will remember you
When the charcoal of evening meets the ebony of night
I will remember you
At all other times
I will simply remember

THE MOVING PICTURE

I LOVED MY FATHER EVEN THOUGH HE TOLD ME OUR FAMILY HELD A DARK SECRET.

The only child of an only child of an only child for as far back as my father knew. He had told me that when he passed away the burden would be mine to carry. I would not have to worry or be weighed down with it till the time came.

Now in my late fifties, able to retire without the proceeds of my father's will and a daughter of my own with a son. I was about to flower and enjoy my retirement early.

A divorce brought on as my husband wanted more children and I was unable to bear any more children.

My father said it was a blight upon our family for generations.

Opening the front door to my father's house brought memories flooding back, that one forgets. A smell, a noise, or even the touch of a long-forgotten item that had been in the family and long forgotten conveys a recollection as if it were just yesterday.

I loved my father and he said as I grew up I should accept and love people for what they are, not what you want them to be. It is still with me and I have passed this on to my daughter and she to her son.

The house, or rather cottage, that my father lived in since his parents had died was small and charming as you would expect of a cottage untouched for years. Two bedrooms with low wooden beams an unhealthy five feet eight from the ground – you were always liable to knock your head. which was extremely likely on the narrow winding staircase around the chimney.

My father had left the cottage in trust to me and my descendants, in perpetuity. Plus all the fittings which had to remain the same. No work could be undertaken to change the structure or layout of the cottage. Although plumbing, electrics and the like could be undertaken, but within the confines of the original structure.

The solicitor had said the will was straightforward. A few small bequests to friends and charities. The remainder, which was a quite substantial, more than I ever believed my father had. Also that I had to live in the cottage as my main home to inherit the proceeds of my father's will. Which I am more than happy to do.

There was never any doubt that I would be here as I fell

in love with it from an early age.

Thatched roof, roses around the doors. wisteria climbing the walls. Even a wishing well in the front garden, which people used to throw coins in and make a wish. To top it all at the end of the rear garden a babbling brook, that gently meandered along its border.

Mr Lang from Height & Lang had also given me a small padded envelope that my father had said should be given to me on his death.

Sitting on a wooden bench in the back garden facing away from the cottage and looking towards the brook, I opened the package and the contents emptied onto the bench – a key and a piece of paper dropped out. A small insignificant key but it looked old. The note simply said:

Do not think evil when evil is around.

The key was large and old and similar to the front door key, though I had never set eyes on it before. I assumed it was as old as the cottage.

Throwing the key onto the note so that it would not blow off the bench, my thoughts were on a cup of tea which I had put the kettle on for ages ago.

Eventually bedtime beckoned as it had been a tiring day, mentally and physically.

Winding my way up the narrow staircase, running my

hand along the wall behind me, feeling the the plaster's curves around the chimney and all the undulations and layers of whitewash seemed to install a feeling of belonging inside of me.

I slept well that night, so well in fact that I did not rise till gone eight o'clock the next morning, when the postman's van drew up outside and as he walked along my gravel path I could hear every footstep.

Making my first pot of tea of the day and two slices of toast with Marmite on, I gazed out of the kitchen window and watched the sun come over the trees beyond my babbling brook. I had forgotten how magical this cottage was.

Going outside, sitting on the bench and drinking my tea, I felt the early morning rays of sunshine on my cheeks. My hand found the key and the note that I had left out by mistake the previous afternoon.

I read it again. 'Do not think evil when evil is around.' I put it back in the envelope with the key and tossed it on the work surface as I walked through the kitchen to the bathroom.

There it stayed until I moved eventually out of my suburban three bedroomed semi into the cottage three months later.

My name on the envelope being in direct sunlight through the window had faded but my note and key were still intact inside.

Putting it inside the kitchen drawer, I moved bits and pieces from one drawer to another until I was satisfied that it was the correct place to be. Like with many items from my previous house, I had to compromise. No room for the three-piece leather suite, the bedroom suite and other items that were just too big for the rooms.

All in now, if a little squashed, but otherwise comfortable in the knowledge that this was my house, my family's home.

That was six months ago and a couple of seasons had flown by. A fine harvest from the few trees in the garden.

Autumn was upon me and I must get ready for it, I thought out loud. I had done my gardening ready for autumn.

Cleaning had been done from top to bottom, throwing out useless items that I would no longer use.

Carrying a new bedside table around the staircase is not an easy thing. I must say I did well – I only knocked one piece of plaster off the wall. Mind you, I would possibly need a plasterer to repair it.

It was the size of my hand and an inch deep.

After taking the bedside table to the bedroom, I returned to the scene of my crime. Brushing the loose plaster away with a dustpan and brush, I noticed a hole had appeared, in which you could just make out the outline of a hole, a keyhole.

Putting the loose plaster in the bin I retrieved the key with the note from the drawer where it had lain with an assortment of keys, batteries, elastic bands, bottle stops and assorted paraphernalia and take away lists for six months. Wedging myself on the stairs, I held the key between two fingers and attempted to see if it might fit.

It seemed to, but I was unable to turn the key as there was not enough plaster missing for it to turn.

I pulled at the plaster that came away easily, making an almighty mess on the stairs.

This time I could not see clearly as the light at the top of the stairs was casting a shadow of darkness across the hole I had made.

Retrieving a wind-up torch and the dustpan and brush again from the kitchen, I once again sat opposite the hole in the wall – which by now was as big as a box of cornflakes.

The key was still in the hole and I could get to it without any hinderance. The light helped me further as I could now see that it was part of a far larger door or cabinet.

The key was black with age but the mechanism of the lock was true and clicked over soundly as I revolved the key between my fingers.

Pulling the key gently, I could feel it pulling towards the plaster but not moving. Hesitating I relocked

It, not wishing to pull more plaster away from the wall.

Taking the key out I tried to shine the light through the keyhole to no avail as the aperture was far too small.

'Sod it,' I said to myself, 'there's always tomorrow and I have a fine mess here to clear up.'

Days passed before I had the time to give it another thought. Interest piqued when I watched a programme on the telly about hidden treasure. I think I made my mind up there and then to search the next day.

Fumbling through the drawer I once again retrieved the key and note, after sticking myself with several sharp and pointed items.

Pushing the key in and hearing the mechanism turn, I pulled at the key. Apart from a large cracking noise and a piece of plaster the size of my toilet seat falling onto my lap, it nearly came open.

As the stairs were now coated in a fine white dust and bits of plaster, there seemed no reason to stop pulling hard at the key. All the edges broke away in a non-uniform manner, allowing me to open the door partially.

It was about two feet wide by four feet tall. When I eventually managed to pull it open after moving down the stairs to allow it to swing open fully, I peered into the dark abyss hoping to find a stash of gold coins or perhaps a few fine pieces of ancestral jewellery.

Nothing so fine other than what looked like a tea tray size object wrapped in greaseproof paper and tied up with string.

Hoping that something valuable lay behind it, I quickly pulled it out only to find not a thing other than plaster dust.

Wiping the dust from my clothes and extracting myself from the stairs, I sat in the kitchen with the object on the table.

Now it is one of those things – do you open it quickly and be disappointed, or open slowly and dream of a lost work of Monet?

It took me almost five minutes to untie the knotted string holding it together; I timed myself by the clock above the stove.

Letting the loose ends of the string fall down the sides of my legs landing in a lump on one shoe, I gently pulled back the greaseproof paper that was all brown and curled at the edges.

To reveal a picture – well, a sort of picture, I think. It was wooden backed, a dark wood probably mahogany, and a simple glass front with a beading around.

Totally white background with people running and walking around in it. Yes people, well I think they were people. 3D drawings but lifelike and moving without any movement of the frame by me.

I sat an interminably long time just staring at these figures moving in the frame.

They were all dressed differently, Elizabethan, Georgian, Victorian, Edwardian and up to the modern day – well recent times anyway.

There were about twenty in all – I could not count exactly as they kept moving around in no particular fashion. Some up or down, others sideways. When passing one another they would doff their caps or nod to one another if they had no hat as they passed each other.

Occasionally one would disappear off the end of the scene, only to appear on the other side to the dismay of the others in the picture.

Well you cannot call it a picture, a diorama would be a better explanation of it.

No one in the picture acknowledged me and why should they – it was only a diorama.

Noticing something written on the paper, I removed it to see if I could decipher any of it.

Do not think evil when evil is around.

This was in italic writing an inch tall, the same as my father's note with the key.

My father had never explained anything to me or of any burden that may come with it.

I began to stare at the figures darting all over the diorama more intensely now, with my head getting closer and closer to the glass frame.

Not being able to see them more clearly, I lay the diorama flat on the table and searched through the drawer for a magnifying glass I knew was in one of them.

Finally finding it, I looked in amazement at the diorama – the people looked almost real.

I had no idea how it was working as it was too thin to have a clockwork mechanism inside.

To my horror I recognised one of the small people: it was an exact lookalike of my nan.

Watching it was all time-consuming as your eyes feasted on the different people.

Then a man dressed in a sailor's uniform began to jump up and down, trying to get my attention, or rather I thought he was.

Now I cannot lip read but I am certain a few oaths came from between his lips.

As if in unison they all began to stop and look in my direction. They either shook their fist at me or umbrella or anything else they may have had in their hand, in a gesture of defiance or anger.

Putting the magnifying glass down next to the diorama, I made my way to the kettle for a cup of Earl Grey.

Sitting at the table, drinking my tea, I picked up the magnifying glass and stared at one of the figures again.

It was my father.

How could that be? So lifelike and shouting something that could not be heard this side of the glass.

Eventually I made out his words.

Do not fear evil when evil is around.

At that moment I knew my fate when my time was to come.

I would join my forebearers for eternity wandering in a diorama.

I put the picture back in the wall and plastered it myself.

My daughter would one day see me again after death, in miniature and join me for all eternity.

I can only assume that at one time a long forgotten relative of mine had made a pact with the devil or a magician.

I know my fate – do you know yours?

? /

DEEP DESPAIR

A lake of deep dark water
Do you fight it or go under
Do you swim or sink
Is a life belt suitable
Do you strive to survive
Or do you sink to defeat
When the beat is gone do you revive it
Do you let it sink to the dark
depths of the blackness of water
so deep, unimaginable as your
eyes close for the final time
Or do you open them and survive
to see the day rise from the blackness of night
Do you falter with excuses
or make amends with the frailties of unconsciousness
Subtlety is not a strength
but a weakness to be explored by others
like defeathering a chicken while it is still alive

ENRIQUE'S GLASSES

Braden could not complain; he had recently divorced. There were no children involved so it was amicable enough. That's how he found himself at Aunt Elsie's.

Elsie was Braden's mother's sister and felt that after the divorce, as her sister had died two years earlier, it was her duty to offer a roof over his head until he could sort himself out.

Braden had been living at Elsie's for five months now and the relationship between Braden and Aunt Elsie was becoming a little strained to say the least.

John, Elsie's husband, felt more and more of Elsie's time was being taken up with Braden's needs.

It was not true, Elsie kept telling John. "You keep blowing it out of all proportion," Elsie told John.

Braden could hear them argue at night and early morning through the bedroom wall.

His simple solution was to stay out as much as possible so as not to cause too much friction between his aunt and uncle, until he could find a place within his limited resources.

This itself caused friction as Braden invariably found himself in the local tavern until closing time, whereas his aunt and uncle normally went to bed after News at Ten.

"Time, gentlemen please." Roddy rang the bell for last orders, as the pot boy filled the bar with empty glasses and crisp packets.

Braden drank the last drop from his tankard. 'Shall I or shall I not…' Putting the tankard down he thought not. Walking to one side of the bar and picking his coat up from a chair and putting it on, he called, 'Night Roddy' then he opened the door to leave. 'Night,' Roddy replied not looking at who he was replying to.

It was only a five-minute walk home over the common, ten minutes around it.

Being fortified by four pints of Benedictine Thumper bitter, the Tavern's guest ale of the month, Braden decided to take the short cut across the common, hoping that he could get in by eleven thirty to see the late film on the telly, as he knew that they would both be asleep and the front room would be his.

In his haste and in no little way to the alcohol he had consumed, he tripped and fell over at the first thing that threw itself at him.

In this case it was a tree root hidden below leaves the tree had shed.

After withdrawing leaves from his mouth which had started to have a residue of dew on them – or so he hoped, as a good few dogs were walked on the common – finding something funny in the situation, Braden pulled himself to his feet and rubbed the dirt and leaves from his trousers and coat that were sticking to him. He brought his hand up to his nose to smell just in case.

Whether it was fate or an accident Braden will never know. He kicked something with his shoe which flipped in the air and he caught it by instinct.

Not wanting to be late for the film, Braden walked on as he looked at what he had caught. Hoping it was nothing to do with dogs.

Seeing they were a pair of old black sunglasses, his arm went back to throw them. Whether it was the drink or the need to get home, he will never know, but instead he put them in his pocket, thinking his aunt may want them.

Getting up late on Saturday was not normal. The norm was up at eight, out as quick as possible, unless there were any chores his aunt wanted doing.

The local greasy spoon for a fry up and then a little shopping, well window shopping and people watching. Then to football if Charlton were playing at home.

If not, then back home to hopefully watch some sport on the telly and see the football results with his uncle after a few swift halves.

Not far from his aunt's house, Braden remembered the glasses. Taking them out of his pocket, he studied them.

They were thick and black and very much like the frames Michael Caine wore as Harry Palmer in The Ipcress File, way back in the sixties. Coming back into fashion now I would expect.

On each side of the frame in what looked like gold was written the word Enrique.

The lenses were as black as the ace of spades. Instinctively Braden put them on but then took them off almost simultaneously, so no one thought he was a little stupid in October to be wearing sunglasses.

Looking around to make sure no one was watching, he put them on again.

He found himself murmuring the immortal Michael Caine words 'Not many people know that' in the best Michael Caine accent he could muster.

A boy cycled past him at speed, gradually drawing away down the path.

Braden stopped as numbers flashed up before his eyes. Two numbers then a further two numbers then four more.

10 04 38

Taking the glasses off and rubbing his eyes then replacing the glasses as a lady appeared from the corner shop.

08 11 42. The numbers disappeared as the lady turned the corner.

Taking them off again and rubbing his eyes and the glasses again, he replaced them on the bridge of his nose.

'No numbers,' he thought, 'I must be going barmy and imagining things.' Taking them off he put them back in his pocket.

Whilst they were sitting waiting for the final scores on the telly, his aunt brought Braden and John a cup of tea and a sandwich on a plate, with a serviette.

Getting up and going over to his coat, Braden fumbled in his pocket for the glasses. He took out the glasses and asked John what he thought of them. Giving it a cursory glance and saying 'not a lot', John returned to watching the telly.

Braden stared at John; the numbers were again showing

on the lenses. He took them off and wiped them with the serviette his aunt had left with the sandwich.

Putting them back on and watching the telly, no numbers appeared. As he shifted his hand to the left and turning to speak to John the numbers appeared again. 17 12 28. Moving his head back to the telly, the numbers once again disappeared.

Aunty Elsie interrupted his attention, diverting his gaze as she entered the room, picking up the empty plates to wash.

The numbers changed; 19 01 49 flashed on the lenses. He gazed back at John and the numbers went back to 17 12 28 .

After a few seconds that seemed like an eternity Braden realised the numbers were like a clock. Looking more closely, Braden could see that below these numbers and smaller were hours and minutes on the left eye lens, and seconds on the right.

Taking the glasses off and making a hurried retreat to his room, he sat on the end of the bed and looked in the mirror and said to himself, 'What the hell have I got here'.

Feeling his heart racing and thumping as he put the glasses back on, he looked in the mirror.

'28 02 20 – today's date,' he thought. The other numbers read 00 00 19 and were decreasing by the second.

18 17 16 15 14 13 12 11 10 9 8 7 6 5 4 3 2 1 0.

Braden's heart stopped at that second the clock ran out. He must have known as he was trying to take them off when his heart finished pumping.

They say your mind carries on thinking for a few seconds after death as long as there is blood moving in your brain.

I wonder what Braden was thinking!

Printed in Great Britain
by Amazon

80837636R00037